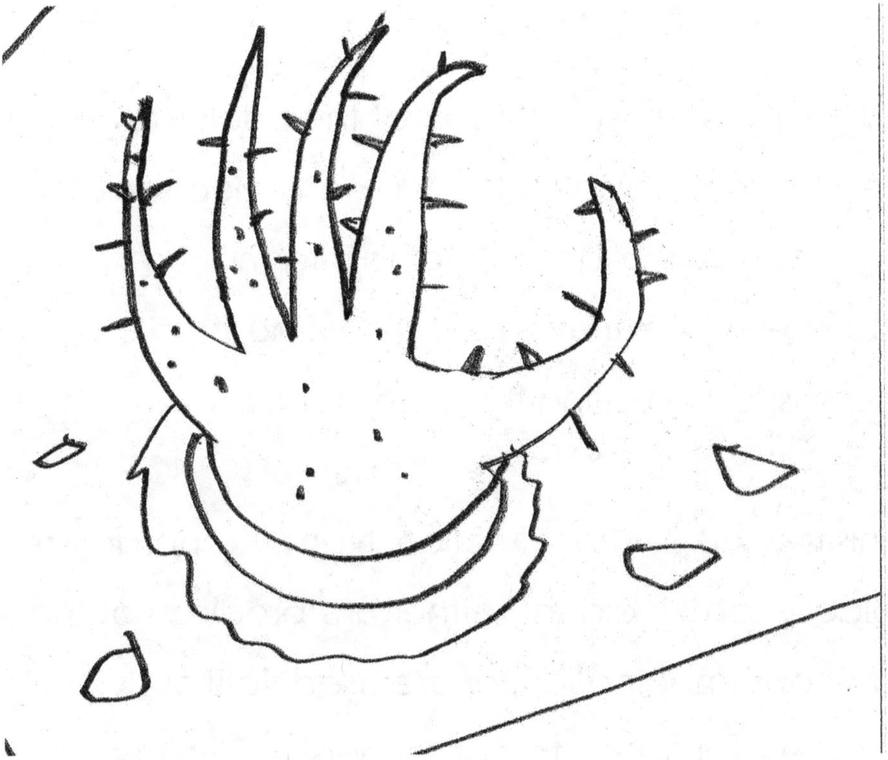

The Creepy Hand

A monstrous creepy hand?

A town being terrorized by a ghost?

A famous writer is taking the blame?

Can three kids figure out what's going on, and clear the author's name?

I would like to thank my brother Nick, my Grandmother and her pets, my Dad for helping edit my book, and my Mother for her encouragement. My Uncles, Aunts, and Cousins who support me. I would also like to thank Clay Ball and his wife Tabitha and their two daughters Savannah and Kasee, Katie Howland and her kids Noah and Emma, Kyle Jurek and his kids Ben and Allie, JD and Megan Morris and their kids Caroline, Braden, and Charlotte, Michael Morton and his family, Patrick Autry and his family, Amber Adams and her family, Sheryl Moriarty and her family, and all my friends who encourage me.

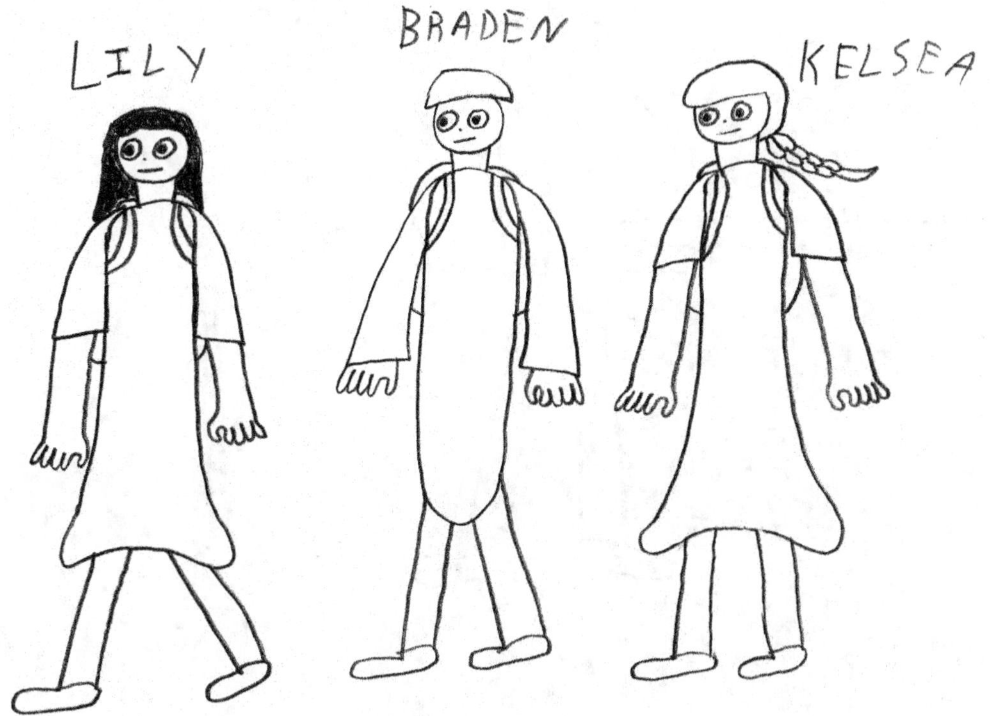

Three kids Braden, Lily, and Kelsea were walking to school. A special guest was coming over and they wanted to get there on time.

The special guest was Mitchel King. He was an author and a storyteller. He made some presentations of his books, and the kids asked him to tell a scary story.

1(Mitchel)

I am going to tell you the story of The Creepy Hand.

2(Kids squeal excitedly.)

Years ago, in this very town, a wealthy man was elected mayor.
This new mayor was very greedy. To him it wasn't enough to be
elected. He wanted more.

The new mayor decided to become a crook, and he started taking everyone's belongings. Nobody in town knew the Mayor was the crook, at least not yet.

An inventor had a new invention hidden in a safe. The Mayor planned to steal it and pass it off as his own. But unknown to the Mayor, the safe was booby trapped. It was charged with high voltage.

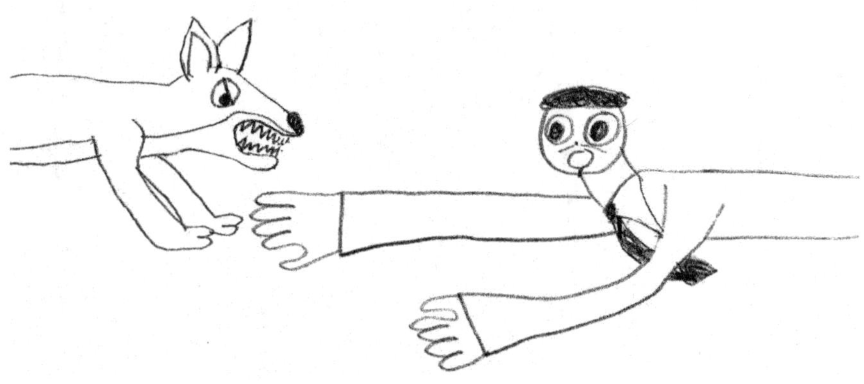

An alarm went off, and the Mayor made a run for it. He ran into the woods and encountered a few wild animals: a bat, a wolf, and a fox. Believe it or not, all three of them bit his electrocuted hand.

As the police were on the Mayor's trail, he tried to make a getaway by climbing over a fence, unaware that it was electrified. The Mayor was shocked a lot worse than he was by the safe. He was taken to the hospital, and vanished the next day.

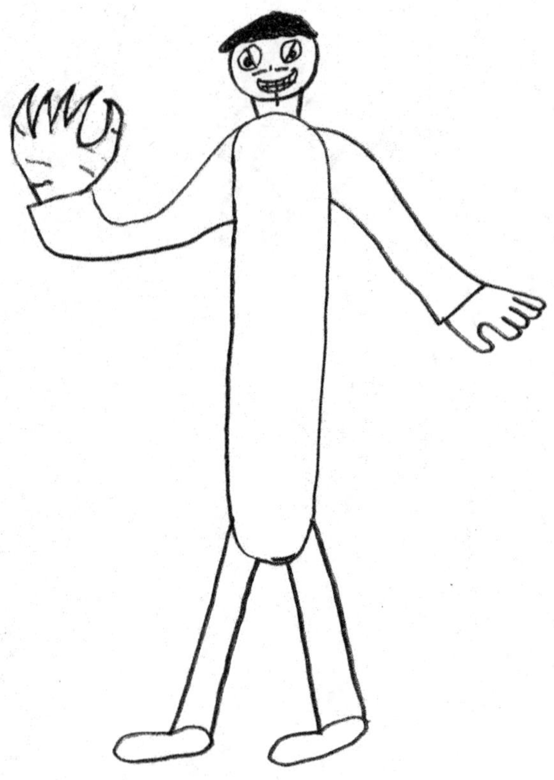

The electricity and DNA from the animals' bites somehow caused the Mayor's hand to mutate, and he liked it. He believed his hand would be very useful.

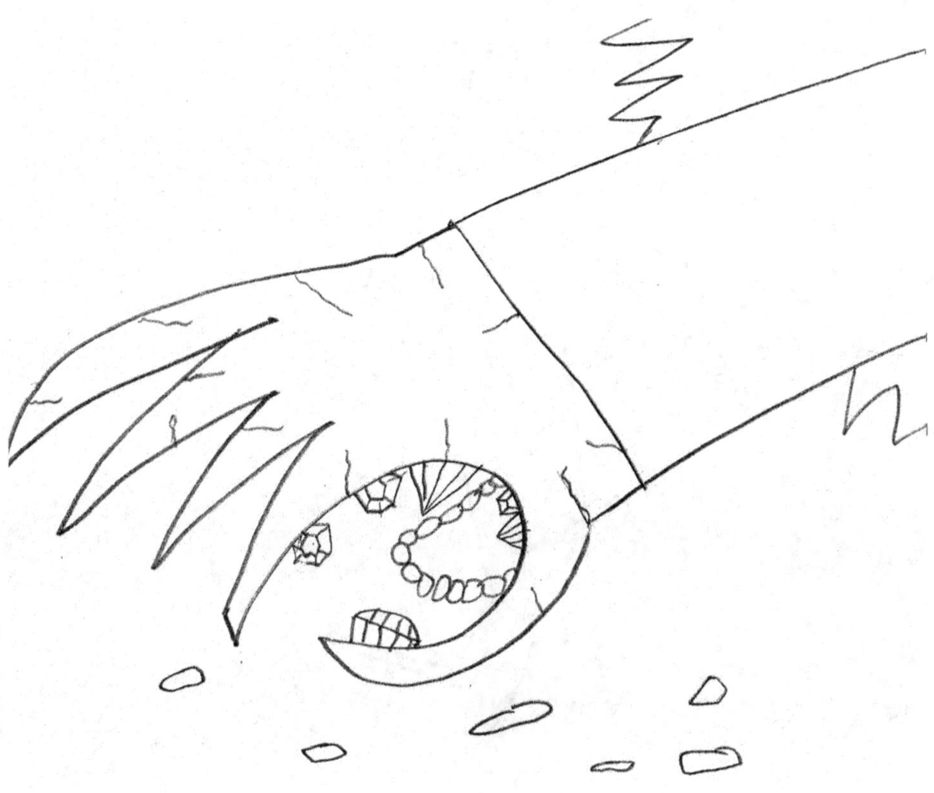

The Mayor used his creepy mutated hand to steal money, jewelry, and a lot more.

The Mayor used his creepy hand so many times it put a lot of pressure on him. His body couldn't handle it, and it became rendered useless. In other words: The Mayor died.

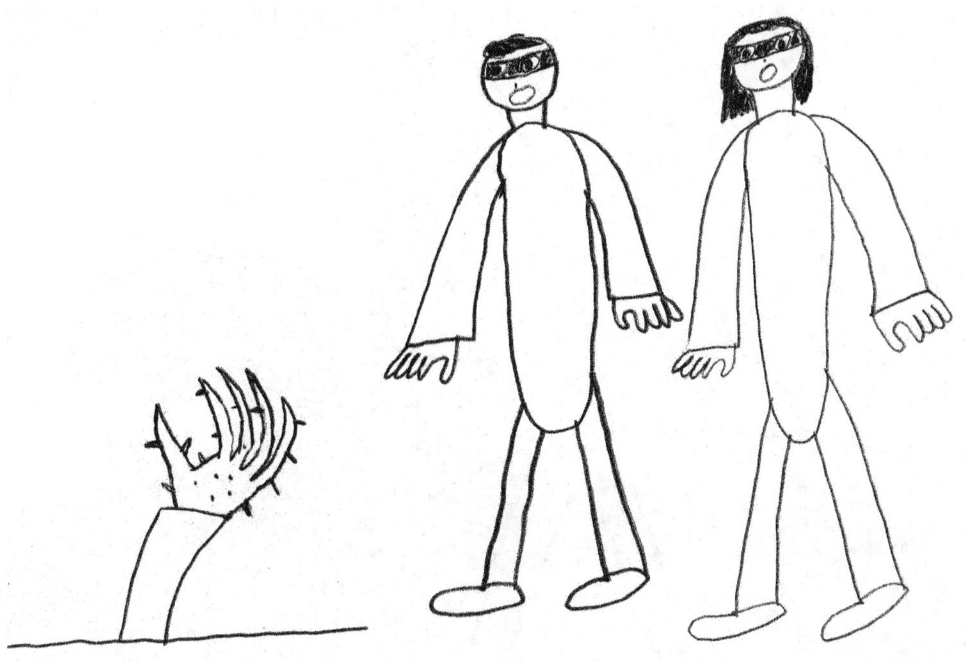

Two robbers heard about the creepy hand. So they tried to dig up the Mayor's grave and take it, only to disturb the grave, causing the hand looking creepier than before, to burst out of the ground.

People have claimed to have seen the Mayor's ghost. They say he became a phantom. It is said he haunts this very town every Friday the 13th at night, taking everyone's valuable possessions with his creepy hand. So look out; the Creepy Hand can pop out when you least expect it.

The kids liked the story of the Creepy Hand. Braden pretended to be it, and walked towards Kelsea and Lily. They both squealed, then all three of them laughed.

A man everyone calls Coach M. told the kids to stop, and says that Mitchel King is a bad man.

1(Coach M.)

I know Mitchel King. He causes nothing, but trouble. He pulls a lot of stunts to sell his stories. Trust me, I know.

After school, the kids went over to Braden's house.

1Braden)

Do you two believe
what Coach M. said is
true?

2(Kelsea)

I have no idea. Others told
me Mrs. C. said the same
thing.

3(Lily)

I had Mrs. C, and
she's a meanie.

4(Kelsea)

Come to think of it, I've
heard both Coach M. and
Mrs. C were bullies when
they were in school.

1(Braden)

I can't believe, Mitchel King would do such a thing. I have a lot of his books. He even signed one of them

2(Lily)

Well, he is a best selling author, and I wouldn't be surprised if someone would be jealous of him.

Suddenly, the kids hear a scream in the distance.

The kids ran towards where they heard the screaming. When they got there, something creepy popped out of some bushes. It was a hand, and it went back into the bushes.

1(Braden)

Could that have been, the Creepy Hand?

2(Lily)

That's what I was thinking.

3(Kelsea)

Me too.

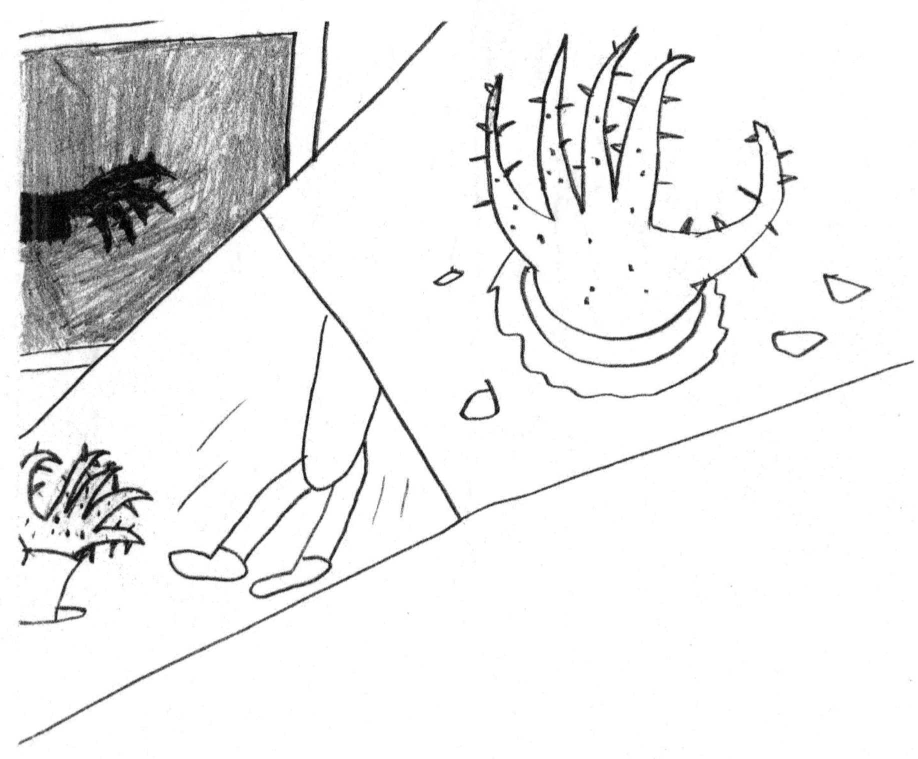

Soon, people all over town were screaming. The Creepy Hand was seen through windows, popping out of sewers, and busting through gates, walls, doors, ceilings, and floors.

 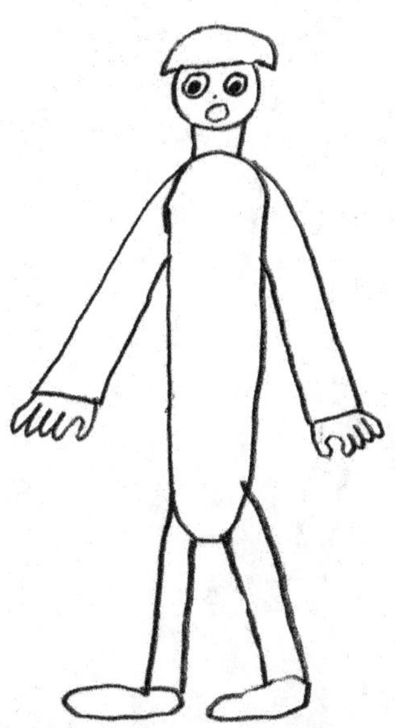

Braden was watching the news, and he saw Coach M. saying that the Creepy Hand is one of Mitchel King's publicity stunts to get people to buy his books, and that he's a cheat. Braden didn't like what Coach M. was saying, and believed he needed to do something.

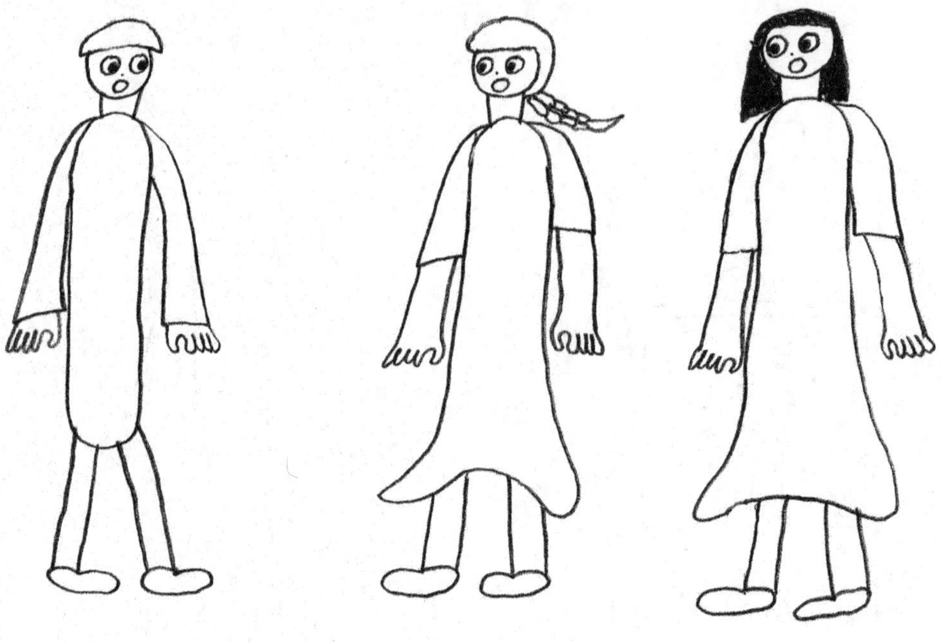

Braden met with Kelsea and Lily. They all saw the news.
They thought about going over to talk to Mitchel King,
but Lily said it was probably not a good idea.

1(Lily)

Where Mitchel King is staying, a
bunch of reporters are over
there trying to interview him,
but he won't come out.

2(Braden)

Well, Kelsea and
Lily, there is only
one thing to do.
We need to
search for clues.

Braden suggested the first place to check was the sewers. He and his friends snuck out at 11:00pm, and arrived at a pothole.

1Kelsea)

Braden, you can't be serious about this?

2(Braden)

People said they saw the Creepy Hand pop out of the sewers. We have to do this for Mitchel King.

3(Lily)

Searching for clues, or Ninja Turtles?

4(Braden)

Very funny, Lily.

The kids went into the sewers. They saw so much filth, and it was really stinky. They hoped to find a clue fast, so they can get out of there.

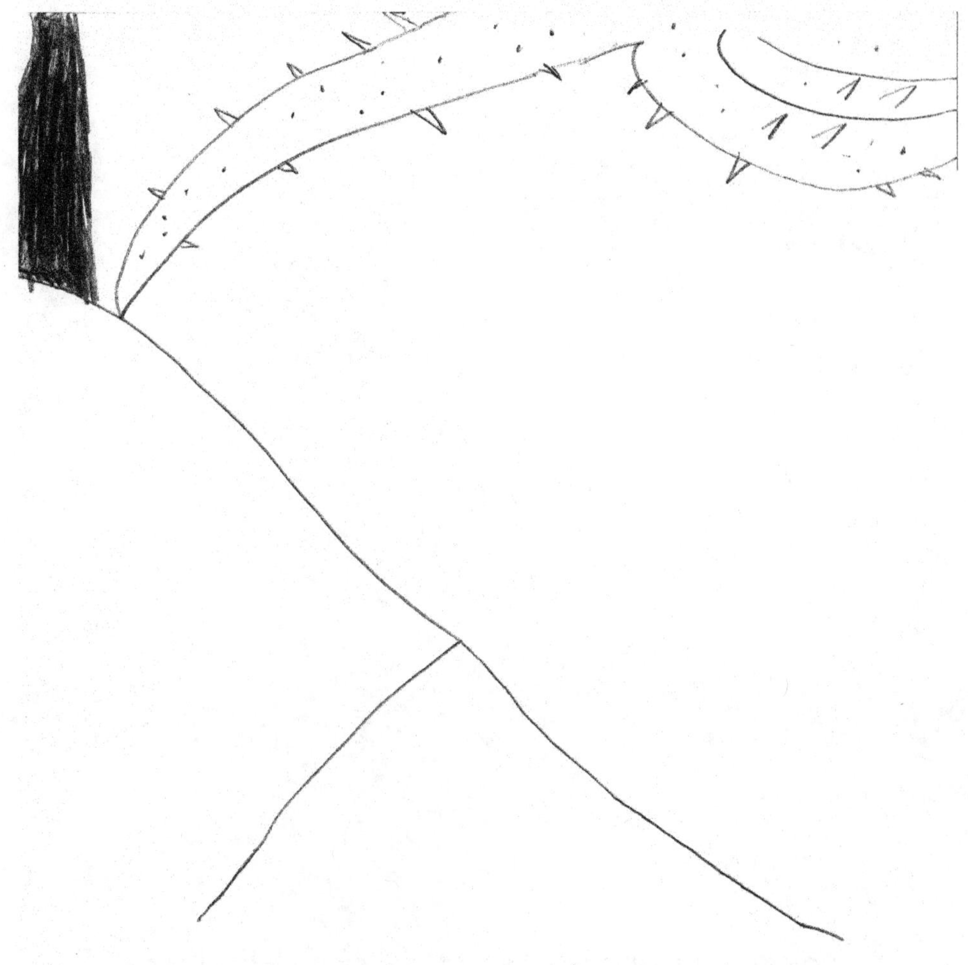

While searching for clues, Lily felt something tapping on her shoulders.

1(Lily)

Who's tapping me?

2(Kelsea)

Not me.

3(Braden)

Wasn't me, either.

The kids turned, and they saw the Creepy Hand! The hand began approaching them. Kelsea and Lily wrapped their arms around Braden so tight, he could barely move his arms.

1(Kelsea)
Let's get out of here!

They got out of the sewers. The kids began panting, and were relieved they lost the Creepy Hand.

1(Lily)

That was a
close one.

2(Kelsea)

Yeah. "Go in the
sewers at night."
Brilliant.

3(Braden)

Hey, we made
it out alright.

4(Kelsea)

Just barely.

5(Braden)

Well, at least
we didn't fall
in any filth.

6(Lily)

Well, I guess
it can't get
any worse.

Suddenly, something creepy appeared right in front of them. Braden says to Lily, "You were saying?" The figure looked like some kind of phantom and had the Creepy Hand. The kids were saying to each other, "Is this the Greedy Mayor's ghost?" Kelsea says, "Never mind that now, let's get out of here!" Then Lily says to Kelsea, "That's the second time you said that! So let's go."

The kids try to make a run for it into the woods. The
Phantom used the Creepy Hand to slash through
branches, and he went after the kids.

1(Phantom)

You kids can run, but
you can't hide from me!

The kids ran as fast as they could to try and lose the Creepy Hand, but it was still on their tail. It also made a bunch of scratches on so many of the trees and left a lot of marks.

The kids ran out of the woods and towards the playground. There was hardly any place to hide. The only place they saw that seemed like a good hiding spot was the playground equipment.

The kids climbed the equipment, and hid as far down behind the walls as they could. But somehow, the Phantom knew where they were.

1(Phantom)

I know you kids are up there!
You're not the first kids to
hide from me there.

The kids managed to escape. They stopped running, because they saw Coach M. and Mrs. C. in the distance with a man they were not familiar with.

1(Stranger)

I got the Creepy Hand prop right here.

2(Coach M.)

Good. Once we pull this off, Michel King will be out of the author industry.

3(Mrs. C.)

Soon he will be famous no more, and we will be rid of him.

The kids heard their plan. They realized they're trying to frame Mitchel King. Coach M. and Mrs. C. turned and saw the kids. The kids made a run for it, and Coach M, Mrs. C, and the stranger chased after them. They caught the kids and decided to frame them, too, as Mitchel King's accomplices.

Suddenly the Phantom appears. Coach M, Mrs. C, and the stranger were terrified, especially at the sight of the Creepy Hand.

1(Phantom)

You three dare to frame innocent children? And that hand of yours is absolutely pathetic. Now let the real Creepy Hand show you how it's done.

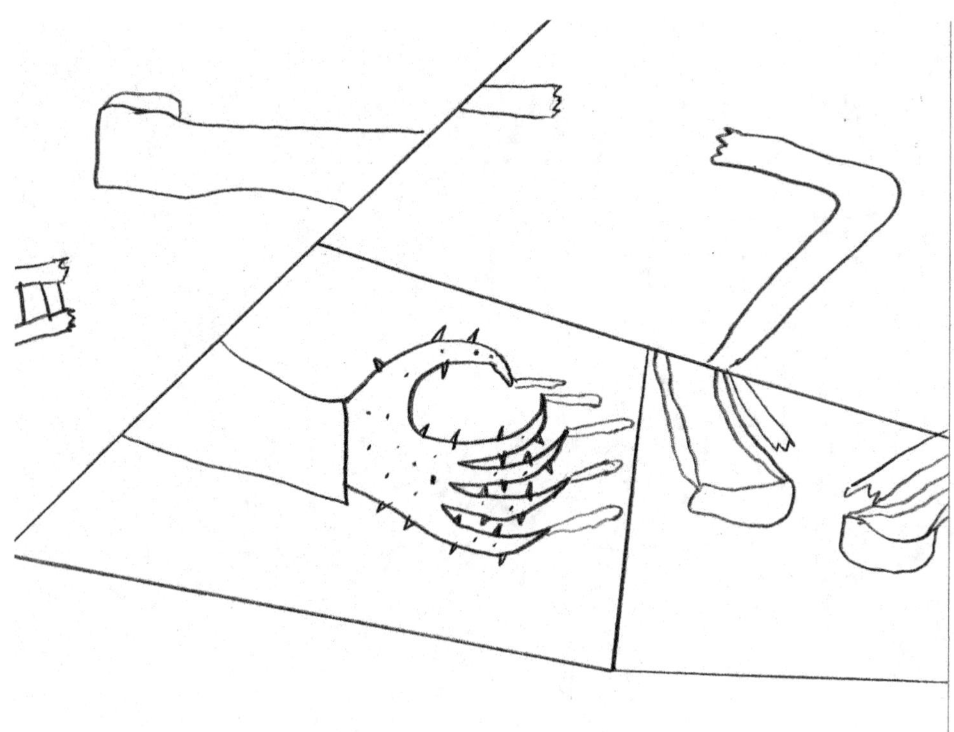

The Phantom used the Creepy Hand on every equipment on the playground, tearing them apart. Coach. M, Mrs. C, and the stranger fainted. The Phantom turned towards the kids, and began chasing after them again.

The Phantom chased after the kids through town. He used the Creepy Hand to slice the streetlights, fire hydrants, telephone poles, smash windows, scratch up vehicles and even make them crash. The Phantom approached the kids, and they were so terrified. But before he got any closer to the kids, they all heard a clock go off.

1(Phantom)

Well, what do you know? Looks like time has run out. See you the next Friday the 13th.

2(Braden)

Did y'all see that?

3(Kelsea)

Yeah, he vanished into the mist. But how?

4(Lily)

We can wonder that later. We need to get back home.

5(Braden)

Good idea. Our parents won't be happy if they see us gone.

6(Lily)

And we better hurry. I think I hear police sirens.

7(Kelsea)

Well, third time's the charm. Let's get out of here!

Coach M, Mrs. C, and the stranger were conscious again when the police arrived. The police saw the Creepy Hand prop next to them, and a lot of damage at the playground and through town. They took Coach M, Mrs. C, and the stranger into custody, believing they caused it, and realizing they tried to frame Mitchel King.

The police announced what Coach M, Mrs. C, and the stranger did on the news. The kids met with Mitchel King and asked why they would try to frame him.

1(Mitchel)

I went to school with them, and they often gave me a hard time. Coach M. and Mrs. C. are what you call, "Partners in bullying," and the stranger is Mrs. C's cousin. They got into so much trouble and started blaming me for it. They don't like the idea of me being famous and an author. They've been trying to make me look bad so other people would avoid me.

The kids went over to Braden's house. They talked about how jealous Coach M. and Mrs. C. were of Mitchel King. They were also baffled about the Phantom, and the Creepy Hand.

1(Braden)

You two don't think that was really a ghost do you?

2(Kelsea)

I have no idea. But the scary thing is, today is Saturday 14th.

3(Lily)

And yesterday was Friday the 13th?

4(Braden)

Oh, boy. Let's not talk about this to anyone, and keep it to ourselves.

5(Lily)

Well, it's not like anyone would believe us if we did tell them.

6(Kelsea)

Some things are better left untold.

The kids decided to play tag. Braden was it. He pulled out his hand and said, "Look out! The Creepy Hand is back." Kelsea and Lily smiled, and screamed. Then all three of them ran.

THE END!

Books by Ian Thomas (available from Amazon)

T-Rex in America

Monster in the Manor

The Thing at the End of the Woods

The Jackrabbit and the Jerk

The Swamp Ghost

The Creepy Hand